The Big Game

by
Gilles Tibo

illustrations by
Bruno St-Aubin

Scholastic Canada Ltd.
New York Toronto London Auckland Sydney
Mexico City New Delhi Hong Kong Buenos Aires

Scholastic Canada Ltd.
604 King Street West, Toronto, Ontario M5V 1E1, Canada

Scholastic Inc.
557 Broadway, New York, NY 10012, USA

Scholastic Australia Pty Limited
PO Box 579, Gosford, NSW 2250, Australia

Scholastic New Zealand Limited
Private Bag 94407, Botany, Manukau 2163, New Zealand

Scholastic Children's Books
Euston House, 24 Eversholt Street, London NW1 1DB, UK

Library and Archives Canada Cataloguing in Publication

Tibo, Gilles, 1951-
[Nicolas, joueur étoile. English]
The big game / by Gilles Tibo ;
illustrations by Bruno St-Aubin ;
translation by Petra Johannson.
Translation of: Nicolas, joueur étoile.
ISBN 978-1-4431-1943-6
I. St-Aubin, Bruno II. Johannson, Petra III. Title.
IV. Title: Nicolas, joueur étoile. English.

PS8589.I26N48813 2012   jC843'.54   C2012-901466-4

6 5 4 3 2 1   Printed in Canada 119   12 13 14 15 16

For two gifts from heaven,
Maéva and Anaïs.
— *G. T.*

For Charles and Antoine.
— *B. St-A.*

Nicholas was lying in bed, dreaming that he was on a warm tropical beach.

Suddenly, his dad barged into the room, yelling, "Hurry! Hurry, Nicholas! Wake up!"

His mom rushed into the room next,
shouting, "Nicholas! I made your lunch!"

Then his sister ran in and jumped on his bed, saying, "Nicholas! I made you a good luck charm!"

His dad started giving him advice before
Nicholas was even out of bed. "Dress warmly,
Nicholas. Arenas are often chilly."

"Yeah, yeah, Dad…" he answered sleepily.

At breakfast, his mother said, "Eat up, Nicholas! You need your energy. You're facing the best team in the league today!"

"Yeah, yeah, Mom!" he replied.

While he was brushing his teeth, his dad kept on. "Don't forget, Nicholas, you need to keep the ice in front of your net clean. Concentrate, cover your corners and remember your peripheral vision!"

Before leaving the house, his mother handed him
a water bottle, his lunch box and more advice.

"Nicholas, don't forget to eat and stay hydrated.
Make sure your skates are tight and that your
helmet is done up properly. Remember your
shoulder and knee pads, too!"

"Yeah, yeah, Mom!" said Nicholas.

On the way, Nicholas's father told him about all the best NHL games. He described every single winning goal in every single Stanley Cup final. He explained the famous Canada–Russia hockey series to him in great detail. Nicholas's head was OVERFLOWING with hockey.

At the arena, Nicholas slipped into the players'
dressing room. While they got ready, the coach
told the team all about their opponents:
   "Number 16 — a real bully!
   "Number 22 — he can't turn right.
   "Number 64 — likes to elbow.
   "Number 44 — careful, he's a scrapper!"
   The team was so scared that every player
was frozen in place.

Coach showed everyone the game plan.
He drew the players and explained all
the plays the team should make.

Ten minutes later, the board was filled with pictures and arrows, dotted lines and directions. Nicholas and his teammates didn't understand a thing. Suddenly, his stomach hurt. His throat was tight. His head ached.

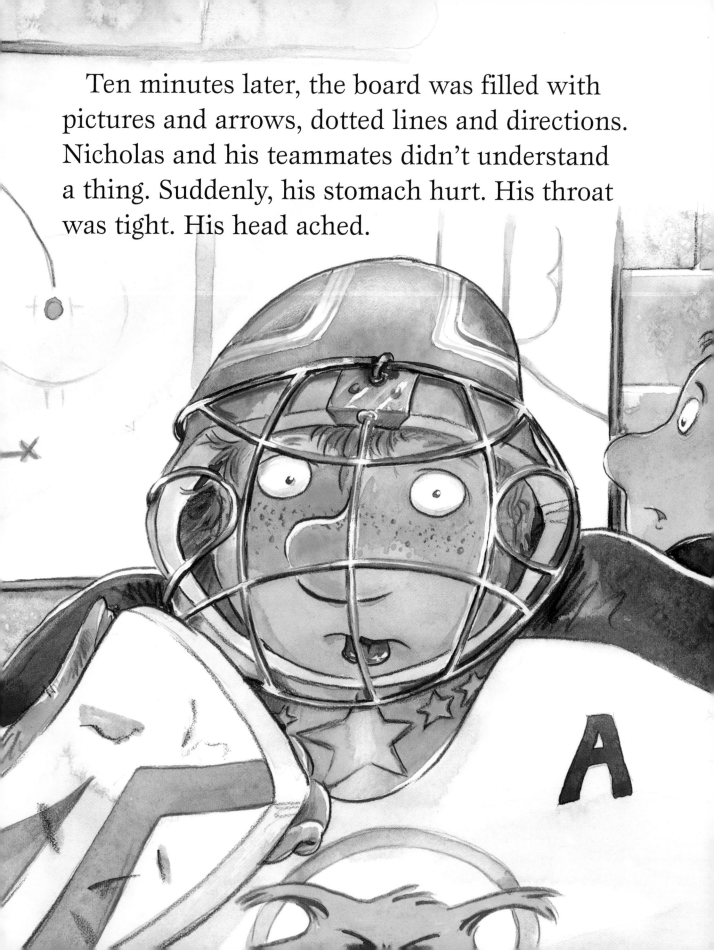

Their heads filled with lines, arrows, stick men and plays, Nicholas and his team hopped on the ice. The arena was overflowing and the crowd was wild. As Nicholas skated toward the net, all he could hear was people yelling.

As he neared the net, Nicholas heard his dad call out, "Come on, Nicholas! You're the best!" 17

The referee dropped the puck and the game began.

Moms and dads, brothers and sisters, aunts and uncles, grandfathers and grandmothers shouted out advice:

"Faster, Sebastian, faster! Score!"

"Max! Keep the puck! Keep the puck!"

"Hurry, Luigi! Pass the puck! Pass it!"

"Paolo, what are you doing?"

It was impossible for the players to concentrate. Both teams were playing worse and worse. Nicholas's defensemen were like sieves, letting every puck through.

Behind him, Nicholas heard his dad yelling: "Be careful, Nicholas. On your right! No, your left! Raise your stick! No, go down low! No, no, no! Stand up! Watch out in front of you! No, behind the net!"

Nicholas was so overwhelmed by all the advice, he couldn't concentrate. By the end of the first period, the other team was ahead by five goals. What a disaster!

Between periods, the players rushed to their dressing room. The coach was furious! He drew another game plan but none of the players understood a single thing.

Nicholas had had enough. His stomach ache was getting worse. He went to the washroom — and he came up with a genius plan!

Nicholas hopped back onto the ice. While the crowd shouted, while the coaches yelled, while the players got more and more worked up, Nicholas was calm. Nicholas was cool. Nicholas was serene.

His defensemen were still letting shot after shot get past them, but Nicholas's concentration was unbreakable. He stopped every single puck. No one could score on him.

Between the second and third periods, Nicholas shared his master plan with his teammates. One by one, each team member went into the washroom and walked back out wearing a huge smile on his face.

In the third period, despite all the noise, despite all the yelling, despite all the mayhem, Nicholas's team was calm. Nicholas's team was cool. Nicholas's team was serene. They passed the puck with such precision, they scored TEN goals.

At last the game was over. Nicholas's team
had won 10–5! All the players were smiling.

Pictures were taken, video was shot,
but when asked about the game, no one
on the team answered.

More and more questions were asked,
but still none of the players replied.

That's when Nicholas and all his teammates reached up and removed their ear plugs!